TRY SATAN

HOW ONE MAN OUTWITTED THE DEVIL, MISPLACED HIS WIFE, & BROKE THE WHEELS OF FATE

DENNIS LOGAN

TRY SATAN: How One Man Outwitted the Devil, Misplaced His Wife, and Broke the Wheels of Fate

First Edition.

Published by **Penemue Media LLC**
Richmond, Virginia, USA

ISBN: 978-1-964297-77-4

This edition of *Try Satan* is a modern literary work blending historical fiction, mythopoetic reflection, and symbolic theology. All characters, names, dialogues, and events are presented in a fictional, allegorical, or metaphorical context. Although inspired by real historical periods and social conditions in the American South, this text is **not** a historical document. Any resemblance to actual persons, living or dead, is coincidental or used symbolically within an imaginative framework.

Library of Congress Control Number: Pending
Printed and bound in the United States of America.

Publisher's Note

Try Satan is presented as a "found manuscript," merging early-1900s storytelling with themes of spiritual negotiation, American mythology, and metaphysical satire. It is not intended as doctrine, ritual instruction, or a literal metaphysical treatise. Rather, it is offered for contemplative reading, narrative exploration, and reflection on the cycles of oppression, agency, belief, and liberation. The manuscript's voice, its devil, and its revelations exist within a literary reality—and the truths they touch must be discerned by the reader.

DEDICATION

For my children,
who will inherit a world of broken scripts
and trembling machinery.
May you learn to rewrite the story
instead of repeating it.

And for the ones who walked before me—
seen and unseen—
I heard you.

TRY SATAN

How One Man Outwitted the Devil, Misplaced His Wife, & Broke the Wheels of Fate

Being the Confession & Instruction of One Elijah Booker, Late of Southampton County

Composed 1877.
Found 2025.

As Received By
Dennis Logan
The Honorable Scribe

Editor's Prefatory Note

The following manuscript was delivered to me by Mr. Horace J. Pendleton, Attorney-at-Law, of Petersburg, Virginia. The envelope bearing my name had rested in his office safe for more than forty years.

The instructions were written in a hand foreign to him:

"Wait for the one who puts the Bible back together."

Mr. Pendleton, now eighty-four and near blind, told me the man who entrusted him with this—
one *Elijah Booker*—
died in late autumn of 1983, a year before my birth.

The pages were brittle, the ink browned, the spelling inconsistent. But the voice was unmistakably conscious, clever, and—to my astonishment—absolutely aware of me.

What follows is transcribed as faithfully as possible.

TRY
SATAN

Being the Statement of Elijah Booker

Recorded for whoever God or Fortune sends to read it next.

Prologue
In Which I Meet the Gentleman

I, **Elijah Booker**, born enslaved on the banks of the Nottoway River, being of sound mind though doubtful spirit, do here set forth the truth of my arrangement, which some will call blasphemy, and others will call common sense.

I was but a barefoot boy when **NAT TURNER** rode the counties like a judgment comet. I saw the flames, heard the screams, and later peered through the slats at Turner himself when he was brought to trial—calm as any Sunday preacher, though the whole world shook on his account.

Now, I loved the Lord then—best I knew how—but I could not help noticing that for all Turner's zeal,
God had not delivered him.
He let the man hang just the same as any common thief.

So when, some twenty years later, a tall pale gentleman in a waistcoat finer than any I had ever seen stepped into the clearing behind my boarding-house and tipped his hat to me, I did not faint nor run.

He smelled faintly of tobacco and library glue.

"Good evening, Mr. Booker," he said, smooth as butter. "Allow me to introduce myself. I was present at the Turner trial as well, though unseen. I believe you have questions."

I should have run then.
But the devil never looks the way Sunday sermons say.

This one looked like a Cleveland lawyer and sounded like a man offering insurance.

"Sir," I said, "I don't traffic with spirits."

He smiled as though he had heard that a million times.

"Oh, but Elijah—why not conduct an experiment?
You saw what the Almighty gives His zealots.
Would you not—simply for fairness' sake—try SATAN?"

He said it like a man says **"try the cheese."**

"If God allows tests," he went on, "then surely the other party must
be permitted one trial as well.
For the record.
For balance."

And because I was tired of plowing fields that would not feed me,
and churches that promised Heaven while landlords raised the
rent, and because the world seemed so determined to stay wicked
without ever improving the lives of the poor—
I agreed.

Just to see.

Just to try.

He shook my hand with a grip cold as courthouse marble,
and said:

"Let us improve your circumstances."

Chapter I
In Which My Circumstances Are Improved Beyond All Reason

The next morning I found a telegram on my doorstep informing me that a position had opened at the VIRGINIA STATE BANK & TRUST.

A *colored man* in a bank in 1877—imagine!
Even I laughed.
But the telegram insisted I report at once for examination.

The examination consisted of an elderly clerk saying:

"Mr. Booker, we are delighted to have you."
(Though he had never met me before in his natural life.)

By week's end, I had a suit, a desk,
and a salary that could make a man polite.

Two months later, I had a wife too— *Miss Adelaide Green*, with parasol, pearls, and eyes like polished walnut. She confessed, after we wed, that she had dreamed of me for months, a strange thing considering we met in the train station that very spring.

The pale gentleman with the library-glue scent reappeared at my doorstep the night I brought Adelaide home.

"Well done," he said. "Now, Elijah,
let us see what a loyal man may rise to."

Within a year, I was ushered into state offices through back doors and unmarked halls, into rooms where white men smoked cigars and talked about the future of entire counties like they were parcels of hog meat.

They called me **Coordinator**.

They put files in my hands containing secrets— about railroads, about schools, about the "colored question," about the new science of "crowd psychology," and the methods by which a people may be trained to hold themselves down while believing they are pulling themselves up.

And the pale gentleman whispered:

"Let them do the work for you, Elijah.
Chains are expensive, but dreams are free."

Thus began my education.

INSTRUCTION I
On the Systems Men Build to Keep Themselves Small

The reader—whoever you are—is warned:

men do not always need masters.
give a man the *idea* of a master, and he will police his own chains.

these are the chief devices by which souls are made obedient,
though no whip touches their backs:

promise them tomorrow
nothing is more effective than hope without plan.
a man with hope will labor twice as hard as a man under threat.

teach them to imitate their oppressor
if the lowest among you longs to be like the highest,
he will defend the ladder that crushes him.

convince them their defeat is personal
make societal burden feel like individual failure,
and no man will revolt—he will simply despair.

give them small successes
a bone tossed to a hungry dog keeps him from looking at the butcher's
shop.

let them oppress one another
once they learn to discipline each other,
the work is done and the cords are self-tightening.

teach them reincarnation without liberation
tell them life is a cycle, but not how to break it.
they will return again and again,
paying debts they never owed.

The Pale Gentleman Taught Me All This, AND I WAS PAID HANDSOMELY TO STUDY IT.

Chapter II
In Which I Become a Functionary of the Invisible Machine

The first thing a man learns, upon entering the lower chambers of government, is that government has no chambers.

Not *really.*

There are offices, yes—
oak-paneled rooms, brass spittoons, telephones that ring only for the right hands. But the true workings lie in the **spaces between the rooms**, in the conversations had behind closing doors, in the ledgers that are never entered in official books.

I became, as they called it,
a **Functionary Without Portfolio**—
which is a fine way of saying a man paid to do things that must not be traced to the men paying him.

My responsibility was threefold:

1. To observe men.
2. To predict men.
3. To persuade men to behave as though the world were arranged precisely as we wished it to be.

This is the art of governance.

But the pale gentleman—whom I now suspected to be no gentleman at all— taught me something deeper:

"Elijah, the world is not ruled by force, but by **suggestion**.
A strong arm can move a man, but a strong idea can move a nation—even if the idea is foolish."

He gave me documents, stamped with seals I had never seen:

THE BUREAU OF PUBLIC TEMPER
THE OFFICE OF EXPECTATIONS
THE COMMITTEE FOR ORDERLY ASPIRATION

I asked if these were real offices.

"Real enough to keep the trains running," he said.

My first assignment was small:
a short report on why poor farmers voted against the very roads
that would have helped them bring crops to market.

I concluded, naïvely, that they did not trust the state.

He *corrected* me:

"No, Elijah—
they trusted *hope* more than infrastructure.
They believed a miracle would come sooner than a paved road."

And once I understood that, I began to see how a people,
when left to their own devices,
can be more reliable **oppressors** of themselves
than *any* tyrant with a whip.

INSTRUCTION II
To Effectively Game & Control the Common Man

These methods were taught to me directly by the pale gentleman, and though they are wicked, their workings are plain:

1. Give Men an Enemy They Will Never Meet
A distant foe is most effective.
It cannot be questioned, shaken, or disproven.
A man will fight a fantasy harder than he will face a fact.

2. Give Them a Hero They Cannot Become
Men will toil twice as hard to reach an unattainable role
as they will for a realistic one.
The unattainable is the sweetest carrot.

3. Replace Shame with Pride
Tell a man his suffering makes him noble,
and he will guard the very chains that choke him.

4. Let the Majority Believe They Are the Minority
Loneliness breeds obedience.
No one revolts if he thinks he is revolting alone.

5. Teach Them to Distrust Their Own Eyes
The man who doubts his senses
becomes the slave of whoever narrates reality.

6. Reward Them for Policing Their Neighbors
A man who informs on a friend feels important.
Importance is the cheapest currency of control.

7. Tell Them History Is a Cycle—
But Keep the Mechanism Hidden
Let them believe "things just happen."
Men who do not know how history works
cannot imagine how to stop its turning.

These lessons I wrote in a notebook given to me,
bound in black leather, stamped with the year 1877,
though I swear I saw digits flicker like lantern-light—
as though the thing recorded years not yet lived.

Chapter III
In Which the Devil's Favor Comes Due

Success, reader, is a strange poison.
Sweet in the mouth,
warm in the blood,
fatal in the end.

My wife Adelaide began to notice changes in me—
shifts in my temperament,
coldness in my speech,
a fondness for long walks at dusk from which I returned
smelling of cigar smoke
and some other odor I cannot describe except to say
it was like a library where all the books whisper at once.

"Eli," she would say, touching my cheek,
"you look at me as though I am a memory you cannot quite place."

I loved her—
but the pale gentleman told me:

"Love is the enemy of ambition. And ambition, Elijah, is the only
virtue your new employers care for."

At night I began having dreams—
not the harmless sort,
but the kind that leave a mark on the waking world.

In these dreams I saw **wheels within wheels**,
great turning mechanisms beneath the earth.
Each wheel held the faces of souls—
not bodies, but faces—
turning, turning, turning through generations.

Some smiled.
Some screamed.
Most simply spun.

When I awoke, I would find soot on my fingertips
and the scent of machinery on my clothes.

Adelaide grew afraid of me.
And though I wished to comfort her,
I found that the part of me that had once sought comfort in another
had hardened—
like a river freezing from the bottom up.

One night she whispered:

"Eli… what did you trade to get this life?"

I could not answer.

The pale gentleman answered for me,
standing in the doorway though I had not heard him enter:

"He traded **nothing**.
He is merely taking the test the Lord declined to grade."

Instruction III
On the Machinery of Reincarnation,
as Demonstrated to Me in a Vision

*(This instruction appears in Elijah's hand,
but the ink is darker here, as though written all at once.-THS)*

Understand this, reader:

Men do not reincarnate because they sin.
They reincarnate because they **believe** they must.

The wheel is not a punishment.
It is a habit.

All souls are caught in three gears:

1. The Gear of Desire
What you cannot release,
you will return to pursue.

2. The Gear of Fear
What you dread,
you will return to confront.

3. The Gear of Debt
What you believe you owe,
you will return to repay—
even if no creditor exists.

Break these three gears and you break the wheel.

This the pale gentleman taught me—not to save me,
but to show me that the world itself is a machine,
and most men are content to be cogs
so long as someone calls them "important machinery."

Chapter IV
In Which I Am Shown the True Face of My Benefactor

It happened on an evening so warm the frogs sang psalms in the ditchwater, and the moon hung over the pines like a pale judge leaning forward to hear testimony.

I had just returned from Richmond, where I'd delivered a report on "community temperament"— a polite term meaning *how long the people will endure the conditions we assign them.*
Men in suits nodded soberly at my findings, as though oppression were arithmetic and a man's spirit a column of figures to be balanced.

When I reached my porch, Adelaide was gone.

The kettle still steamed.
Her sewing lay open on the chair.
A single glove lay on the steps,
fingers curled as though reaching back toward the house.

I called her name. The walls gave no answer.

Only then did I notice the pale gentleman sitting on the porch swing, pushing himself gently back and forth with the toe of a spotless shoe.

He held a newspaper folded to the society section,
but the printed letters crawled across the page like ants,
rearranging themselves in patterns that hurt my eyes.

"Good evening, Elijah," he murmured.
"You look troubled."

"My wife," I said, "is missing."

"No," he corrected,
"she is *moved.*"

He gestured toward the yard, and I saw—
for the first time without dream-haze—
the machinery beneath the world.

The soil breathed.
The shadows bent at curious angles.
And between the rows of corn in the neighbor's field,
dark metal glinted:
gears tall as men,
turning slowly in the earth,
each spoke etched with faces like the ones from my nightmares.

The wind did not move them.
The earth did not resist them.
They turned as though time itself were the engine.

"My God…" I whispered.

He laughed—
the first true laugh I had heard from him,
and it was nothing like a man's laugh.
It was the sound of a train whistle blown backward;
it was the creak of ice splitting on a lake;
it was the noise grief makes when it escapes the throat.

"Elijah," he said,
"You have spoken His name very freely for a man in my employ."

I stumbled backward.
"What have you done to Adelaide?"

"Adelaide is safe," he replied,
"but she does not belong in this chapter of your story.
You wished for advancement.
Advancement requires simplicity.
A wife is complexity."

I surged forward, fists clenched,
but he raised one gloved finger,
and the air thickened around me
as though I had stepped into honey.

"Elijah," he said with a gentleness worse than cruelty,
"You must stop taking the world so personally.
You are part of a much older arrangement."

With his free hand he removed his hat—
a small gesture, one any polite man might make—
and beneath it his face shimmered.

Not changed.
Shimmered.

His skin peeled away like wet paper.
His features rearranged
as though an unseen sculptor pressed clay through a mesh.
For a moment I saw nothing but light—
cold, white, surgical—
and then the light folded itself into a shape
my mind could not hold straight.

It was not monstrous.
It was worse.

It was familiar.

A face like mine.
But paler.

Older.
More amused.

A face that knew every failure of my bloodline
and every hope of my descendants
and found both equally entertaining.

"Elijah," it said—
and the voice no longer came from the mouth,
but from the ground beneath my feet—
"I am not your enemy.
I am merely the administrator of consequences."

I felt my knees go weak.
The shadows around the porch lengthened,
reaching outward like ink poured on cotton.

"You asked what happened to Nat Turner," the thing continued.
"What happened is what always happens:
**men choose trials they are not prepared to pass.
You chose mine.**
And you are performing admirably."

I wanted to curse, to pray, to denounce,
but every word tasted like betrayal of someone—
my wife, my ancestors, myself.

"Where is Adelaide?" I managed.

He replaced the hat.
His face snapped back into its human mask
as easily as a man closes a pocketwatch.

"She is where all loved ones reside

when a man *chooses* **power** *over* **peace**."

He stood and offered me his hand again.
The same cold marble grip.

"Come, Elijah," he said,
"there is more to learn.
And very little time left for ignorance."

He led me off the porch
toward the cornfield where the gears turned beneath the earth,
their great faces passing slowly like saints in a blasphemous
procession.

I FOLLOWED.

*Because what else can a man do
when the devil finally stops pretending
and starts teaching?*

Chapter V
In Which I Am Shown
the Architecture of the Wheel

The cornfield parted for him.

Not by wind, nor by any earthly movement,
but as though the stalks remembered the pale gentleman
and stepped aside out of long habit.

The gears below the soil—
those titanic wheels I had glimpsed only in dream—
rose now in full view.

Great iron halos,
each taller than the steeple of Mount Zion Church,
turned without friction or sound,
their spokes carved with faces in every expression the human soul
can invent:

Joy.
Terror.
Hatred.
Hope.
Weariness older than pyramids.
And a blankness I recognized as the expression of men who believe
life is simply "the way things are."

"These," the pale gentleman said,
"are the **Wheels of Continuance**.
You call it reincarnation.
Others call it destiny.
I call it *administration*."

He rested his hand on a massive spoke.
The metal did not burn him nor cut him;
it greeted him like an old colleague.

"Observe, Elijah," he whispered.

A face rotated into view—
a woman's face, eyes wide in terror—
then it passed and another took its place,
then another,
and another,
until the motion blurred them all together.

"This wheel," he said,
"contains every soul bound by **desire**.
All who crave what life withholds from them,
all who chase glittering promises,
all who believe that enough gold, or love, or vengeance
will complete them—
they come here."

I watched the wheel turn.
The metal looked impossibly ancient,
yet freshly oiled with human longing.

Another wheel rose beside it,
this one darker,
its faces twisted in dread.

"And this," he continued,
"is the **Wheel of Fear**.
The coward returns until he ceases to be afraid.
The anxious return until they grow tired of trembling.
The cautious return until they dare."

"And the last?" I asked,
though my throat had gone as dry as gunpowder.

A third wheel emerged—
not of iron, but of a dull bronze
that reflected nothing.

The faces on its surface looked defeated,
resigned,
as though forever apologizing for existing.

"This," he said,
"is the **Wheel of Debt**.
Every man who believes he owes the world repayment—
for his survival,
for his color,
for his father's sins,
for the land he walks on—
they are bound to this one."

I trembled.

"And Adelaide?" I whispered.

He smiled—
a small, courteous smile,
like a banker explaining a declined loan.

"She is not bound to any wheel," he said.
"She is simply... put aside.
Until your test is complete."

"And what test is that?"

He stepped closer,
and the corn around us rustled though no breeze blew.

"Elijah," he said softly,
"You are to write the manual."

"The manual?"

"The instruction for escaping these wheels.
The very knowledge the Almighty never entrusted to His prophets
because He feared what free men might do with it."

He touched his breast pocket.
I heard a faint ticking from within.

"Someone must gather the wisdom.
Someone must articulate the pattern.
Someone must prepare the mind of the one
who will someday put the Bible back together."

I froze.

"You mean—"

"Yes, Elijah.
Your task is preparatory.
Your reader—
the one who finds this lockbox—
is the one who will finish the work."

The devil's smile never widened,
but something behind it did.

"You are the scribe," he said.
"He is the hand."

I staggered backward.

"You expect me to serve you by liberating others?"

He chuckled.
"Is that not the most efficient form of oppression?
Let the slave believe he is freeing himself.

Let the teacher believe he is teaching truth.
Let the liberator believe he is liberated."

He leaned in,
and though his breath smelled of tobacco,
I also caught the scent of burning parchment.

"There is nothing more beautiful," he murmured,
"than a prison a man builds for himself
and calls it revelation."

INSTRUCTION IV
The Seven Ways Souls Keep Themselves Enslaved

*(Written in Elijah's hand,
as though dictated through him.-THS)*

1. They mistake comfort for freedom.
A comfortable man stops asking who profits from his comfort.

2. They confuse movement with progress.
A treadmill is still a machine.

3. They worship suffering as proof of righteousness.
A whipped back does not make a holy spine.

4. They fear offending those who harm them.
A polite prisoner is still a prisoner.

**5. They inherit the nightmares of their ancestors
and mistake them for instincts.**
Trauma masquerades as tradition.

6. They believe survival is the same as purpose.
A man can live long without ever living rightly.

7. They wait for permission to save themselves.
And permission never comes.

Chapter VI
Adelaide's Letter From the Interstice

I did not sleep that night. How could I?
The gears beneath the world hummed like a hive,
their faces turning ceaselessly.

Just before dawn, as the first crack of light split the horizon,
I heard the whisper of paper sliding under the door.

A letter.

My hands shook as I opened it.

The hand was unmistakably Adelaide's— small, looping,
the script of a woman who learned penmanship
before she learned disappointment.

It read:

My dearest Eli,
I write from a place between moments.
I am not hurt.
I am not dead.
I am paused.

You chose a path that does not allow wives to walk beside their
husbands.
I do not resent you.
But I cannot follow you into the machinery.

There are rooms here—
rooms made of memory—
and I am allowed to sit in the one where we first danced.
I hear music from a gramophone that has never existed,
and yet I know the tune by heart.

Eli, you must finish your task.
But do not believe the pale man when he tells you the price is fixed.
All contracts may be amended by the brave.

Find me when the gears stop.

Yours in every life,
Adelaide

I pressed the paper to my chest and felt the faintest warmth,
like the dying ember of a hearth still capable of lighting a fire if tended.

The pale gentleman reappeared behind me.

Touched my shoulder.

Said nothing.

Just smiled.

INSTRUCTION V
How the Oppressed
Become the Oppressors

*(This section appears more neatly written than the others, as if
Elijah's hand steadied with grim understanding.-THS)*

Reader, understand this truth:

Oppression is not a ladder.
It is a **circle**.

Those at the bottom dream of the top, and when they reach it,
they build the same pit they once climbed out of— brick for brick—
because it is the only architecture they know.

Here are the seven transformations by which
a victim becomes a warden:

1. Grievance becomes entitlement.
A man who suffers long enough begins to believe the world owes
him recompense.
The moment he believes this,
he stops fighting injustice
and starts fighting inconvenience.

2. Envy becomes aspiration.
Oppressed men dream not of freedom,
but of switching chairs with their master.
So when the day comes,
they sit exactly as he sat
and wonder why the room feels familiar.

3. Pain becomes policy.
A man will call his own trauma "wisdom"
and inflict it upon the next generation as education.

4. Fear becomes law.
Those who were once ruled by terror
rule others by the same script—
reciting the very punishments they once endured.

5. Scarcity becomes strategy.
Men who once begged for crumbs
become hoarders of feasts
because nothing frightens them more
than remembering hunger.

6. Obedience becomes governance.
Every tyrant was once a child praised for being "good,"
never realizing goodness was measured by compliance.

7. Silence becomes culture.
The oppressed learn to swallow truth.
Later, when they hold power,
they teach others the same diet.

This is the great joke of the wheels,
the devil's favorite symmetry:

Men escape history only to become its authors.

Chapter VII
In Which the Devil Explains the "American Cycle"

The pale gentleman led me back into the yard as dawn softened the sky, and the gears sank once more beneath the soil like leviathans returning to deep water.

He stood beside me, hands behind his back like a schoolmaster proud of an obedient student.

"Elijah," he said, "have you ever wondered why your nation behaves as it does? Why each century repeats the last? Why revolutions age into institutions, and institutions into prisons?"

I said nothing. The letter from Adelaide still burned in my coat pocket.

"This experiment," he continued, "the American one— it is the most exquisite wheel ever crafted."

He began walking slowly, circling the porch as though lecturing a roomful of unseen students.

"It operates on four movements— like a piece of clockwork."

His voice deepened, resonant now, as though it carried the acoustics of a cathedral.

Movement One: Idealism

"The new people arrive.
They believe they are free.
They declare all men equal—
while quietly deciding who qualifies as a man."

Movement Two: Exploitation

"To build their shining city,
they break the backs of those excluded from the promise.
They justify this by scripture,
by science,
by tradition,
by whatever story lies nearest."

Movement Three: Guilt

"Eventually, conscience stirs.
(Not morality—no.
Just discomfort.)
The privileged seek redemption
through committee,
charity,
or symbolic gestures,
but never by relinquishing power."

Movement Four: Amnesia

"Finally, the offspring forget the sins that made their comfort
possible. They call the suffering of others 'unfortunate,'
not 'inherited.' They speak of progress,
not cost. And thus the wheel turns—
back to Idealism again."

He stopped in front of me,
lifting my chin with the tip of one gloved finger.

"America," he whispered,
"is a nation that reincarnates without ever dying."

He stepped back.

"And you, Elijah Booker,
are now part of its maintenance crew."

My stomach twisted.

"I never asked for this."

"*No one does*," he replied gently.
"*That is what makes it such a perfect system*."

Chapter VIII
In Which I Attempt
My First Rebellion

His words hung in the air like funeral cloth.

I felt the weight of every field I'd plowed,
every sermon I'd heard,
every dream I'd been told to abandon.

And suddenly— unexpected even to myself— I spit at his shoes.

A small act. A *child's* act.
But the only act that felt ***human*** in that moment.

He looked down at the spittle. Then up at me.
His **smile grew** slow and *delighted,*
like a cat discovering a wounded bird with ambition.

"Rebellion," he sighed. "*At last.*"

He snapped his fingers.

The world **folded**.

Not crashed, not shattered   folded,
like cloth being refolded by invisible hands.

When I opened my eyes, we were no longer in the yard.

We stood in a vast chamber lit by lamps that burned with cold fire.
Bookshelves spiraled into the distance in every direction.
Columns rose and fell like lungs.
Desks arranged themselves without being touched.

"The Library of What Men Choose," he said.
"All thoughts that ever lead a man astray,
or lead him to greatness—
same thing, usually—
are catalogued here."

I stepped backward,
but the floor moved with me,
keeping me close.

"This," he said, "is where you will write your rebellion."

"I will not help you," I said.

"You misunderstand, Elijah.
I do not wish your obedience.
I wish your **resistance**.
It is far more productive.
Great revelations are born from protest."

He placed a blank book in my hands.

The pages were crisp.
Empty.
Waiting.

"Begin," he commanded softly.

"What am I supposed to write?"

He smiled.

"Write *how* you will **overthrow** me."

I froze.

"***Why*** would **you** ask **me** to **do that?**"

He leaned close,
his breath cold as cellar stone.

"Elijah," he murmured,
"only those who try to defy me
ever learn the truth about me."

INSTRUCTION VI
The Method
for Breaking the Wheels

*(The pages of this section are written in a strange rhythm—long
lines followed by sudden short ones, as if Elijah wrote in one
breath, then caught another. -THS)*

The pale gentleman urged me to plan his overthrow.
I discovered, to my astonishment,
that overthrowing the devil is no different
from escaping one's own habits.

The wheels do not bind the soul.
They mirror it.

To break the wheels
is to break the self
that clings to them.

Here is what I learned,
in that impossible library
where thoughts are catalogued like debts:

1. Name the Story You Are Living Inside.
Every soul is trapped in a narrative before it is trapped in a cycle.
The wheel cannot release a man
who cannot say where his story begins
and whose voice is telling it.

2. Abandon Your Inherited Script.
Your ancestors hand you their unfinished business
wrapped in tenderness and trauma.
To honor them,
you must *stop repeating them.*

3. Refuse the Currency of Fear.
Fear buys nothing but more fear.
Refuse to spend it.
Refuse to earn it.
Refuse to trade in it.

4. Disobey What You Mistook for Fate.
Fate is merely the name we give
to our own lack of imagination.

5. End a Cycle by Completing a Sentence.
Say what was never said.
Feel what was avoided.
Choose what was always left unchosen.
The moment a sentence becomes whole,
the wheel loses interest.

6. Forgive Without Forgetting.
Forgiveness frees *you.*
Memory protects *you.*
Together they unfasten the bolts of the wheel.

7. Walk Away Before You Win.
Fools seek victory.
The wise seek exit.
The moment you stop trying to "win" at life,
the wheels discover they have nothing left to grip.

This is the great secret:
You cannot defeat the devil
by fighting him.
Only by *interrupting the story*
in which he appears necessary.

Chapter IX
In Which I Discover What the Devil Actually Wants

The pale gentleman paced behind me
as I sat with the blank book open on the desk.
His footsteps made no sound—
and yet I felt each one
like a cold fingertip on the back of my neck.

"Write," he insisted.

So I wrote:

*'If I were to overthrow the devil,
I would begin by identifying the need he fulfills...'*

He halted.

His interest sharpened.

"Elijah," he murmured, "be careful.
Truth spoken too plainly is a dangerous instrument."

But I continued:

*'Men make devils to explain the parts of themselves
they are not prepared to accept.'*

His jaw tightened,
but he let me go on.

*'The devil fills the gaps—
the gap between desire and discipline,*

the gap between fear and honesty,
the gap between comfort and conscience.'

The pale gentleman tapped his gloved fingers on the desk, a steady, clicking rhythm, like a telegraph reporting incoming revelations.

I looked up.

"You are not a person," I said.
"You're a **job**."

He blinked— slowly,
like a snake caught in the middle of shedding its skin.

"Explain," he said.

"You are the role men create when they want someone else to carry their responsibility. You are the administrator of consequences because men refuse to administer consequences to themselves."

A faint smile tugged at one corner of his mouth.

"You are not God's adversary," I said.
"You are men's excuse."

Now the smile evaporated.

"Elijah Booker," he whispered, his voice suddenly sharp as sleet, "you tread close to blasphemy."

"No," I said.
"Only close to truth."

I stood, the blank book slipping from my hands.

"You need us to believe in you," I said. "Because without our belief, your job—your *function*— ceases to exist."

He stepped back as though I had struck him.

The lamps flickered.
The shelves shuddered.
The room inhaled sharply,
like a creature wounded.

"Elijah," he rasped, "sit down."

"No."

His eyes glowed— not red, not gold—
but the pale glow of a match just before it catches.

"*You misunderstand your place*," he hissed.

"And you **misunderstand** your origin," I said.

**"If men ever stopped believing in devils...
there would be no devils."**

For the first time since I met him,
he looked afraid.

Not of losing power—
but of losing *purpose.*

The chamber trembled.
Pages tore themselves from books.
Desks spun like carnival rides.

I stood in the center of that storm,
finally seeing the shape of the truth:

The devil wanted rebellion
because rebellion validated his existence.

He needed opposition to justify his office.

He needed men to try and fail so he could remain
necessary.

"Well," I said softly,
"your test is over."

Chapter X
The Bargain Revised

The devil recoiled.

"Elijah," he said, voice cracking like drying paint,
"you forget who holds your wife—"

"No," I interrupted. "You forget. You told me yourself:
all contracts may be amended by the brave."

His expression twisted. Anger, pride, terror, calculation—
all flickered through him like lanternlight
dancing across dangerous water.

"*How will you amend our contract?*" he snarled.

"By **refusing the premise**," I said.

He froze.

"*What premise?*"

"That I owe you anything."

The moment I said it, the entire room stopped moving.

The lamps stilled.
The pages fell silent.
Even the air paused,
as though waiting for the next line.

"Elijah," the pale gentleman whispered, almost gently,
"*do you know what you have just undone?*"

"Yes," I said.
"I have **ended** our **bargain**.
Not by **defeating** you—

but by **withdrawing** my *consent*
to be governed by the story you told me."

A long silence.

Then he sighed. Soft. Tired.
Like an old clerk closing the ledger of a bankrupt business.

"Elijah Booker," he murmured,
"you are either the bravest man I have ever met...
or the most foolish."

He snapped his fingers.

The blank book vanished.

The library collapsed into darkness.

I felt the world shift— fold— turn inside out.

And then I stood again in my yard,
the dawn finally brightening the sky.

The gears beneath the earth were silent.
Still.

Adelaide's glove lay on the step.

But the pale gentleman was gone.

FINAL INSTRUCTION
The Door Out of All Cycles

(This page is written in a slanting, urgent script—less like a lesson, more like a warning.-THS)

Reader— you who have found this, you who arrived at the appointed hour— know this:

The wheels beneath the world *do not keep turning because the devil commands them.*

They turn because **men obey them**.

And men obey them because they accept the **frame** of the world as immutable.

But frames can be **broken** as easily as wood.

Here is the final instruction the pale gentleman never meant me to learn:

1. Question the Frame, Not the Picture.

Your suffering is a picture.
Your circumstances are a picture.
Your history is a picture.
The frame is the story that contains it.
Break the frame—
the picture dissolves.

2. Walk Away From Every Script That Begins With "That's Just the Way It Is."

This is the lullaby sung by tired tyrants and tired ancestors alike.
Do not inherit resignation.
Do not pass it on.

3. Forgive Yourself for Believing the Lie.

The wheels are not powered by sin.
They are powered by **shame**.
Step out of shame,
and you step out of the mechanism.

4. Stop Asking for Permission to Live a New Life.

A man who waits to be allowed to change never does.

**5. Understand: You Do Not Break the Wheel.

You Step Aside and Let It Spin Without You.**
Do not win. Do not conquer.
Do not triumph.
Walk away.

6. Love Without Bargain.

Devils cannot touch love that asks for nothing, expects nothing,
controls nothing. Such love cracks the gears.

7. Tell the Truth About Yourself.

Even the parts you were taught to hide.
Especially those.
Lies are the grease of the wheel.
Truth is the sand.

If you do these things, you will not need to reincarnate to finish this work. You will not need to inherit what your forefathers carried. And the devil— robbed of his job— will have no claim on you.

As for me— I have one task left.

I must retrieve Adelaide.

That is the one wheel I refuse to let turn without my interference.

FINAL TESTAMENT
Addressed to the One Who Receives the Lockbox

(These last pages feel different—steadier than the rest, as though Elijah wrote them with full clarity and no fear.)

To you—
the one who puts the Bible back together—
hear me.

The pale gentleman said you would come.
He said you would be the hand,
and I the scribe.
I am content with that arrangement
so long as you do not become another gear
in the devil's beloved machine.

Every age has its liberator.
Most fail because they try to save a world
that has no interest in being saved.

But you—
you are not here to save the world.

You are here to **understand** it,
then **rewrite its script**.

The wheels beneath the soil
are not your inheritance.
They are your assignment.

You must walk two paths at once:

1. **Expose the machinery**
so others recognize it in their own lives—
2. **And refuse to be caught in it yourself.**

Do not build new prisons
to replace the old.
Do not exchange one tyrant for another—
not even a righteous one.
History grows weary of righteous tyrants.

Speak plainly.
Act quietly.
Love fiercely.
And when the world insists on telling you who you must be—
step out of the frame entirely.

As for me—
I go now to the Interstice,
the place between seconds,
to find my wife,
my Adelaide,
and to tell her
our wheel has stopped spinning.

If this manuscript reaches you,
know that I chose courage at last.

And know—
whoever you are,
whatever task lies before you—
that courage is the one gift
the devil cannot counterfeit.

Remember my instruction.
Remember Adelaide's letter.
Remember the wheels.
Remember to walk away.

When you put the scriptures back together,
do so with gentle hands—
and with eyes that see the machinery beneath the text,
but refuse to bow to it.

I end this account
with the final truth the pale gentleman never spoke:

The devil does not fear God.
The devil fears men who stop believing he is required.

Farewell.

—Elijah Booker
Southampton County
Somewhere between one dawn and the next

EPILOGUE
The House in Southampton

I should tell this honestly,
even if it makes me look like a fool,
because every good revelation begins with a man thinking about
the wrong thing
at the wrong time
in the wrong county.

It was early May, the air thick with that Virginia humidity that
makes even ghosts sweat,
and I had driven down to **Southampton County**
—Turner's land, Booker's land—
for reasons that were not scholarly, holy, or respectable.

In plain words:
I was looking for company.
Adult company.

She lived in one of those sagging country houses that look dead in
the daytime
and twice as alive at night.
Paint peeling, porch light flickering,
yard so quiet it felt like it was listening.

The moment I stepped inside,
the air changed.

Not cold,
not hot—
crowded.

Like a room full of people holding their breath.

The lady smiled and said,
"Don't mind the noises.
Old house."

But the noises were not "old house" noises.
There were footsteps upstairs,
though no one lived upstairs.
A door creaked open down the hallway,
slow and polite,
as though someone wanted to announce their presence
without interrupting.

At one point I walked into the kitchen
and saw a shadow bend around the doorway
before disappearing altogether—
not flicker,
not retreat—
bend,
like someone walking out of sight.

I should've left.
Any sane man would've left.
But temptation and curiosity are cousins,
and neither has ever been polite company.

At some point the lady laughed at something trivial I said,
and for the briefest moment
I swear I heard a second laugh behind hers—
deeper,
warmer,
older.

Not mocking.
Not malicious.
Just... present.

I didn't understand it then.
But I felt it.

Two spirits.
Together.
Kind.
Protective.
Patient.

Watching.

When I left the house that night
—nerves rattled,
desire evaporated,
heart pounding in my ears—
I sat in the car a full minute
with the engine off,
hands gripping the wheel like I was afraid I'd float away.

And I whispered aloud without knowing why:

"Elijah?"

The porch light blinked once.

Just once.

Then went still.

I drove home with the windows down
and the strange certainty
that I had walked into someone else's story—
someone long dead
but not gone.

A Week Later
A Lockbox Arrives

On **May 25**, the day *The Universal Bible* went live,
the day I should have been celebrating,
resting,
smiling at my own accomplishment—
the postman left a package on my porch
addressed in handwriting from another century.

Inside:
The lockbox.
The key.
Elijah's manuscript.

A note in the envelope,
yellowed, brittle, patient:

**"For the one who puts the Bible back together.
Deliver upon the release of his scripture."**

The lawyer's signature was almost faded away.
But I recognized the date:

He had written it decades before I was born.

When I lifted Elijah's pages,
the house in Southampton
—the one with whispers and footsteps and shadows that bend—
rose in my mind like a memory that wasn't mine.

And suddenly,
everything aligned.

**Elijah and Adelaide Booker never returned from the Interstice.
Because they never needed to.**

They stayed where love held them—
in a place between seconds,
in a house where time breathes differently.
As ghosts, yes—
but not lost ones.
Chosen ones.
Protectors.
Spectators of the wheel they escaped.

The house was theirs.
The presence was theirs.
The laugh in the kitchen was theirs.

They had been waiting—
not for a priest,
not for a prophet,
but for a publisher who could hear their story.

And when *The Universal Bible* released,
the timing aligned.

Their task ended.
Mine began.

Closing Note

I realize now that the house wasn't haunted.
Not in the way people mean.

It was **inhabited**.
By a couple who outsmarted the machinery of the world
and chose eternity together
over reincarnation apart.

Elijah wrote the manual.
Adelaide preserved the love.
The lockbox carried the message.

And I—
foolish, flawed, curious, chosen—
happened to walk into their orbit.

So this is the epilogue:

They live happily ever after
not in heaven,
and not in earth,
but in the seam between moments
where the gears cannot turn
and the devil cannot follow.

And they delivered their manuscript
to the one who could finish the work they began.

Me.

AFTERWORD —
On Trembling Doors
and Open Hands

There is a moment, right before a man accepts his calling,
when he looks backward instead of forward—
not because he doubts what he must do,
but because he wants one last glance
at the life he thought he was supposed to live.

Before the lockbox arrived,
I thought my life was a straight line:
work, study, create, raise my children,
fight through the tides of bills and burdens,
sleep a little, pray a little,
try to be a good man in a world that makes goodness feel like a
trick question.

But the truth is simpler:

I was being led.

Not by angels.
Not by ancestors.
Not by fate.

But by **unfinished business**,
older than any name I carry.

And the day Elijah's manuscript touched my hands,
I felt reality lean—
just slightly—
as though someone had tilted the board.

Not violently.
Not forcefully.
Just enough to say:

"Pay attention."

Since then, I've come to understand something that no sermon
prepared me for:

There are doors we walk through knowingly,
and doors we walk through ignorant,
and then there are the doors that open themselves
because generations before us
pushed until their hands bled
trying to make sure that *we*
would be the ones to step across the threshold.

I didn't choose this story.
But I won't run from it either.

Because in Elijah Booker's trembling script
—in his fear, defiance, clarity, and hope—
he left behind a compass,
and every line points to the same instruction:

Break the wheel.
Break the story.
Break the need for devils and saviors alike.

And if the world insists on telling you who you must be,
walk sideways,
walk crooked,
walk laughing—
but walk out of the frame.

There is no destiny but the one you dare to rewrite.
No scripture but the one you have the courage to restore.
No bondage except the stories you refuse to question.

And if you must test something—
if you must see for yourself
whether the machinery runs because you push
or because someone pushes you—

then take Elijah's challenge.
Take his recklessness.
Take his audacity.

Take his dare.

try
SATAN.

SEARCH & FIND OUT

Also Hear These Works in the Voice of Dennis Logan

Over the past decade I have devoted thousands of hours to recording sacred texts, apocrypha, and esoteric classics. If *Try Satan* spoke to you, you can continue the journey through these and many more audiobooks available on Audible and other platforms:

Search "Dennis Logan" on Audible for the complete catalogue of 100+ works across scripture, history, spirituality, folklore, mysticism, occultism, and esoteric literature.

Scripture, Apocrypha & Ancient Texts

- *The Universal Bible* of the Protestant, Catholic, Orthodox, Ethiopic, Syriac, and Samaritan Church
- *Lost Books of the Bible: The Great Rejected Texts*
- *The Book of Jasher*
- Book of Enoch, Jubilees, Jasher & The Book of Giants: The Complete Scriptures of Nephilim & Fallen Angels
- The Books of Enoch and The Book of Giants (featuring 1, 2, and 3 Enoch with the Aramaic and Manichean Giants texts)
- The Book of Jubilees: The Little Genesis, The Apocalypse of Moses
- *The First and Second Books of Adam and Eve*
- *The Kebra Nagast : The Glory of the Kings*
- The Book of the Bee: The Syriac Text
- The Holy Piby: The Blackman's Bible
- The Gospel of Barnabas

Gnostic, Mystical & Esoteric Studies

- *Banned from the Bible*
- *The Gnostic Gospels of Philip, Mary Magdalene, and Thomas*
- *The Gnostic Scriptures*
- *An Advanced Lesson in Gnosticism*
- The Secret Teachings of All Ages
- *The Kybalion, Tablet of Hermes & Emerald Tablets*
- *Thought-Forms*
- *The Initiates of the Flame*
- *The Way of Initiation*
- *Golden Verses of Pythagoras*
- *The Gateless Gate*
- Science of Breath

Magick & Occult Classics

- *The Book of the Sacred Magic of Abramelin the Mage*
- *The Lesser Key of Solomon*
- *An Outline of Occult Science: A Modern Edition*

Myth, Folklore & Religious Narratives

- *Legends of the Yoruba*
- *Aradia: The Gospel of the Witches*

Original Works by Dennis Logan

- *The Pancrotic Sutras of Master Stryfe*
- *The Apocatastasis of Enoch*
- *The Testament of Samson*
- *Try Satan: How One Man Outwitted the Devil, Misplaced His Wife, & Broke the Wheels of Fate*